"Cheer up, Grampa Gloomifjord!"

by Jonathan Wills

with pictures by Martin Emslie

for Alfie, Vašek, Milo and Louie

(with thanks to Kjell and Jorunn)

Some West Norway stories to be read to children by grown-ups

(or the other way around if you prefer…)

The Shetland Times

2011

"Cheer up, Grampa Gloomifjord!"

ISBN 978-1-904746-66-9

First published by The Shetland Times Ltd., 2011

A catalogue record for this book is available from the British Library.

Printed and published by
The Shetland Times Ltd., Gremista, Lerwick,
Shetland ZE1 0PX, Scotland.

Contents

The Rainy Day in Gloomifjord

It was a wet, cloudy Saturday on the west coast of Norway and the Sommerdal twins, Ottar and Brita, were going on the bus to visit Grampa in Gloomifjord with their Mum.

The bus splashed along the Sommerdal valley, up the Hill of Trolls, round the edge of the Helly Woods and was almost at the entrance to the Gloomifjord Tunnel when it stopped.

"Oh dear," said the driver, Mr Murkidal. "Look, the river has burst its banks and washed away the Gloomifjord road. We shall have to go back to Sommerdal."

The road was so narrow there was nowhere to turn the bus. Mr Murkidal had to reverse it almost all the way back. He got a stiff neck, looking over his shoulder all the time. At Sommerdal he parked outside the clinic and went in to see the doctor.

"What are we going to do now?" asked Ottar. "How will Grampa get the cake we made him?"

"Don't worry," said Mum, "We can take the ferry to Gloomifjord instead. She sails in five minutes. Hurry up and we'll just catch her."

The crew were about to pull up the gangway when Mum, Brita and Ottar ran on to the pier.

Captain Larsen was a friend of their Daddy's, ever since they were at the Sea School together. He let Ottar and Brita stand with him in the wheelhouse of the ferry as they steamed down the Sommerdal Fjord, round the lighthouse on the point, past the waterfall and Bog Island and through The Narrows into Gloomifjord.

"Will you just look at the waterfall!" said Captain Larsen. "I haven't seen so much water going over there for twenty years!" The twins went out on deck to look at the amazing cascade where a whole river fell over a cliff into the sea hundreds of metres below. They had their oilskins and wellies on so they were warm and dry despite the rain.

Captain Larsen said: "As we say in Bergen, there's no such thing as bad weather, only bad clothing. And I see your clothes are just perfect for such a rainy day!"

Grampa met them at the Gloomifjord ferry pier. He had a big black umbrella to keep the rain off as they walked along to his house. It was a funny house, built half on top of an old pier at the shore.

"Haa-lo, Grampa!" said Ottar. "You don't look very cheerful."

"Who can be cheerful in this endless rain?" said Grampa. "It's gone on for weeks and weeks and weeks. It's so-o depressing. Come and see: it's flooded the garden and my potatoes are under water so I can't dig them up."

"Cheer up, Grampa, we'll soon see about THAT!" said Brita. She and Ottar ran over to the garden while Mum took Grampa into the kitchen to make him a nice cup of coffee.

The bottom of the garden really was more like a lake. And there were potatoes floating in it.

"What we need is something to dig a ditch with and drain out the water," said Brita. They went to look in Grampa's shed and there they found a spade and a bucket.

Soon they had dug a drain down to the bottom corner of the garden. There they made a big hole and let the floodwater fill it up. When it reached the top, the water cut itself a little channel and splashed happily down over the rocks into the sea.

The twins collected all the floating potatoes and put them in the bucket. Then Brita tapped on Grampa's kitchen window.

"Come and see, Grampa! Come and see!" she shouted.

"Oh what kind and clever bairns!" said Grampa. "This is wonderful! Not only have you drained my garden and rescued my potatoes, but you've made me a boating pond as well!"

Grampa went into his shed. "Just wait a minute," he said. He reached up into the loft and brought down a dusty old model sailing boat, covered in cobwebs.

"I haven't played with this since your mother was a little girl," he said. "Come on, let's go for a sail!"

They sailed the boat on the new pond until dinnertime and rescued lots more potatoes. Then they roasted them in the kitchen stove and ate them with melted butter. And, although it was still raining hard, no one minded a bit.

3

The Gloomifjord Horse

4

It was a dark winter's day when Grampa Gloomifjord rang up about the logs.

"Haa-lo Grampa!" said Ottar. "What's happening today?"

"What's happening is I'm running out of logs for the fire. You remember when the rain washed out the Gloomifjord road?"

"Yes," said Ottar. "We were on the bus coming to see you and we had to turn back and go on the ferry instead."

"So you did," said Grampa. "Well, Hans Tufte's truck was supposed to come with the logs next day but it took weeks to fix the road and he never came and now he's got no logs left to sell to me. So we need to go and find some."

"I'll go and find Mum," said Ottar.

When Mum had finished talking to Grampa on the phone she made another call. Then she told the twins to put on their wellies and warm winter woollies because they were all going to the Helly Woods with Farmer Nils Brattbakk.

Farmer Brattbakk was waiting by his gate.

"Are we going to ride on your tractor?" asked Brita.

"No, my lass," said Farmer Brattbakk. "It's far too muddy and steep for a tractor where we're going today, so we'll do the job the old fashioned way. We'll take the Gloomifjord Horse."

They all sat on the cart. Farmer Brattbakk said "Giddy HUP!" and the horse started pulling the cart up the Hill of Trolls towards the Helly Woods.

"Why's he called the Gloomifjord Horse when he lives with you in Sommerdal?" asked Ottar.

"That's because he was born in Gloomifjord," said Farmer Brattbakk. "He loves to go back there. See how keen he is to climb the hill!"

Soon they were in the woods. Farmer Brattbakk led the Gloomifjord Horse by a halter and stopped next to some trees. He took a big axe from the back of the cart.

6

"See how close together these trees have grown," he said. "We need to thin them out so the big ones can grow better." He started to chop down a tree. When it was ready to fall he called: "Stand well back, everyone!" He chopped once more with the axe and the tree started to move. It creaked, it groaned, it cracked and then it whooshed down to the ground with a loud 'FWHUMP!'

"What do we do now?" asked Brita. "It's too heavy for us to carry."

"No problem," said Farmer Brattbakk. "The Gloomifjord Horse will make light work of this." He unhitched the cart and tied a long rope from the horse's collar to the fallen tree.

Then he said: "Giddy HUP!" and the Gloomifjord Horse pulled the tree over to a pile of logs lying at the edge of the woods. Next to them were some logs that had been cut up into shorter pieces.

"Why are you untying it?" asked Brita. "I thought we were going to pull it all the way to Grampa's House."

"Well, this tree's no use for burning until it's dried out for a couple of years," said Farmer Brattbakk. "These logs here are from trees I cut down earlier. But every time I take logs from the pile I fell a new tree to put in their place. That's the old way, to make sure you never run out of wood for the fire."

They loaded the logs onto the cart and soon they were on the track leading over the top of the hill. When they could see down into Gloomifjord, Farmer Brattbakk stopped and got out his binoculars.

"There! He's waiting for us!" he said. "Do you want to have a look?"

Ottar and Brita took turns to look through the binoculars. They could see Grampa standing by the gate above his garden. He seemed to be very busy with something but they were too far away to see what he was doing, even through the binoculars.

The Gloomifjord Horse went even faster downhill. Farmer Brattbakk let the twins hold the reins as they squelched down the muddy track. When they got to Grampa Gloomifjord's back gate they were all out of breath, even the horse.

7

Grampa had just finished setting up a sawing frame, a chopping block and a bench. On the bench lay a huge saw and two axes, a big one and a small one. Grampa shook Farmer Brattbakk's hand: "Thank you for this. You're a good friend, Nils," he said. "I've got everything ready but first let's find you and that poor horse something to eat!"

When Farmer Brattbakk and Mum and the twins had eaten some brown bread and goats' cheese and drunk some apple juice, they set to work. Brita gave the Gloomifjord Horse a bucket of water and Ottar put some oats in his nosebag for him to munch.

Grampa and Farmer Brattbakk started sawing the logs.

"Can we help?" asked Ottar.

"You can try," said Grampa. So he took one end of the saw and the twins took the other.

"This is hard work," said Brita.

"It's all that, my lass!" said Farmer Brattbakk. So they took turns and quite soon there was a pile of little logs just the right length to fit in Grampa's old Jøtul iron stove.

"But, Grampa, the logs are still too fat to go in the door of the stove," said Ottar.

"Ah, that's where I come in!" said Mum. She picked up the big axe. "I haven't done this for years," she said, and started splitting the logs into thinner ones.

"Can I have a go?" asked Brita.

"Not until you're bigger, dear. An axe is a very dangerous instrument, you know. But you can go and give the horse another drink. He's thirsty after all that work."

"So am I," said Grampa. "Just as well I brewed some Gulating beer last week." And he winked at Farmer Brattbakk, who winked back.

It was dark before they finished chopping all the logs.

"It's too late for you to go all the way back over the Hill of Trolls," said Grampa. "So why don't you stay the night? Nils, you can sleep on the sofa by the fire, and the horse can sleep in the shed."

"Sounds like a good idea to me," said Farmer Brattbakk. "And in the morning we might go back up for some more logs. Did I hear you say you'd brewed some beer?"

When Mum came upstairs to read the twins a story and say "Night, night!" they could still hear Grampa and Farmer Brattbakk in the parlour down below, clinking their beer glasses and laughing.

"What are they laughing about?" asked Ottar.

"Oh," said Mum. "They're just talking about the old days in Gloomifjord, long, long ago when the Gloomifjord Horse's granny was young and strong, and no-one had a snow tractor."

9

The Great Gale of Gloomifjord

It was a windy Saturday in Gloomifjord. The twins were staying with Grampa while Mum went to Bergen on the ferry to meet Daddy from his ship.

"What's for breakfast, Grampa?" asked Brita.

"Well I suppose we could boil some eggs, if the hens have laid any," said Grampa. So the twins went outside to look. Sure enough, there were three brown eggs in the hens' nest box, still warm.

But, just as Ottar was closing the door to the hen run, one of the hens ran out. A sudden gust of wind caught her and whisked her away up in the sky. She flapped wildly in the gale and they saw her land on the steeple of the church.

"Grampa! The black hen's blown away!" cried Ottar.

"Oh, dear, oh dear, oh dear!" said Grampa. "We'd better leave breakfast till later and see if we can get her back." So they wrapped themselves up warm against the cold wind and ran up the hill towards the church.

"Please, have you got Grampa's black hen?" Brita asked the church minister, Pastor Stavkirke.

"Oh, so that's what it is," said Pastor Stavkirke, and pointed at the weathercock. "I thought I was seeing double."

Just then there came another gust of wind. It blew the black hen off the weathercock. She whirled over their heads and down over the harbour.

"Come on, Grampa, let's go after her!" said Brita. They ran off down towards the ferry dock.

"Oh dear, oh dear, oh dear," puffed Grampa. "I'm too old for this cross-country hen running!"

The hen had landed on the mast of the Bergen ferry, which had just come in. The twins and Grampa rushed up the gangplank.

"Please help us get Grampa's hen back," Brita begged Captain Larsen.

"I don't see how," said Captain Larsen.

"If I climb the mast to get her she'll just fly off again. But we'll have to think of something or she'll be sailing all the way back to Bergen with us."

Just then the ship's cook popped his head out of the galley.

"Aye, aye, skipper," he said. "Here's a few scraps for the gulls."

"Wait! Please!" said Brita. "Let's see if the hen will come down to eat them." So they laid the bits of crusty bread and scraps of bacon rind on the deck and, sure enough, the black hen flew down and started to peck. She was so busy eating that it was easy for Ottar to catch her and wrap her up in his jumper.

"Got you, you naughty hen!" he said.

"Now then, what's going on here?" said a big cheerful voice behind them.

"Daddy! It's Daddy!" cried Brita.

"Right first time!" said Daddy. "My ship docked early so we caught the first ferry home."

12

And so they all walked back along the shore to Grampa's for a proper Gloomifjord winter breakfast of boiled eggs and porridge and pickled herring and goats' cheese and crusty brown bread and strong black coffee, while Daddy told them all about his voyage to America.

Later, Grampa gave the black hen a second breakfast, back in the hen run.

"Such kind and clever bairns!" he said.

"I know," said Mum.

13

The Gloomifjord Windylight

On the Sunday night after the black hen blew away, the wind got up even more and there was a great storm. Trees blew down and blocked the road home to Sommerdal so the bus couldn't go. It was such a terrific tempest that the ferry couldn't leave the harbour. So they all stayed another night with Grampa.

Very early next morning, when it was still dark, Brita woke up. She pressed the switch on the bedside light. Nothing happened. She got out of bed and pressed the switch by the door. It stayed dark.

"Ottar!" she whispered. "The lights don't work." Then the twins heard a noise down in the kitchen. As they tiptoed downstairs, feeling their way in the dark, they saw a flickering light through the kitchen door. It was Grampa Gloomifjord. He was lighting candles.

"Grampa, the light in our room doesn't work," said Ottar.

"I know. It's terrible, isn't it?" said Grampa. "The wind must have blown down the power lines up on Trollface Mountain. It's always happening. Such a nuisance." He lit the stove and put the old kettle on to boil.

Daddy came down to breakfast carrying an electric torch. "Windy old morning!" he said cheerfully. "Never mind, though. Every day's good for something, eh?"

"I don't know what good a day like this is to anybody," said Grampa.

"Aha! Just wait and see!" said Daddy.

After they'd eaten their boiled eggs Daddy took Ottar and Brita along to Mr Stord's shop by the ferry dock, where the Gloomifjord people bought all the odds and ends they needed for their boats. Mr Stord sold rope and brass screws and flags and paint and brushes and chain and shackles and saws and hammers and big rolypoly buoys and fenders.

Daddy went into the back of the shop to talk to Mr Stord while the twins played with a big coil of rope and two orange plastic buoys.

15

"Come and give us a hand with these boxes, please!" Daddy called from the back shop. He handed out a long metal pole and five cardboard boxes. Some of them were rather heavy. Mr Stord brought some string and soon he had the boxes slung under the pole so the twins and Daddy could carry them over to Grampa's.

When they got there Grampa was out. Mum had taken him to the old people's lunch at the church hall. Daddy went into the shed to fetch a drill, a hammer and a screwdriver and they got to work.

Ottar held the pole while Daddy fixed it to the end of the house. Then they lowered it down again and Brita opened the biggest of the boxes.

"But what is it, Daddy?" she asked.

"It's what we sailor men call a windylight," he said. "Our skipper has one on his yacht and I reckon if it works on a boat it ought to work on the land."

"But what does it do?" asked Ottar.

"It makes free electricity," explained Daddy. "The propeller whizzes round in the wind and that turns this generator thing that looks like an electric motor which makes the electricity which we store in the battery, here."

They bolted the windylight machine to the top of the pole so it could swing round in the wind. They screwed on some electric wires and then hauled the pole upright again. The propeller started turning at once.

Daddy clipped the ends of the electric wires to the battery and a little red light on the control box went on.

"There you are," said Daddy. "Free electric light. Now let's wire up some bulbs in the house."

When Grampa came home with Mum after lunch and saw the windylight he was as pleased as he could be: "Oh, what kind and clever bairns!" he said. "Now I've got emergency lights even if the wind does blow down the power line on Trollface Mountain."

"We did have a little help, Grampa," said Brita.

17

National Day in Gloomifjord

Brita was telling Grampa Gloomifjord her news on the phone: "It's National Day tomorrow," she said. "It's the 17th of May and we've been practising our singing with the school band. Isn't it exciting?"

"Oh dear, can it really be that time of year again," said Grampa. "Such a lot of noise and fuss."

"Yes," said Brita. "And this year it's Sommerdal's turn to come over to Gloomifjord for the celebrations. We're going to sing the 'Yes, we love our country' song! And Mum's baking a cake with a flag on it!"

"Oh yes, and when does the parade begin?" asked Grampa.

"At the Gloomifjord Pier at two o'clock," said Brita. "Our school's all coming on the ferry. We get in at ten to two so Mum says we'll just see you up at the hall after the procession."

"That'll be nice," said Grampa. "Well, I suppose I'd better go and find the flag to fly from the flagpole on my chimney pot."

"Night night, Grampa," said Brita.

Ottar and Mum were working in the kitchen. Ottar had mixed up the flour and butter and sugar and eggs for the cake. He licked the spoon."Ottar! Wait until it's in the cake tin!" said Mum, as she checked if the oven was hot enough.

"But it tastes so nice raw. It's a pity to cook it!" said Ottar.

"Please can I lick the bowl when you've put the icing on?" asked Brita.

"You can share it with Ottar, you greedy girl," said Mum with a smile. "Look: we've got red, white and blue icing for the cake's flag."

Next morning was dry and sunny for National Day and everyone wore their national dress as they walked down to the Sommerdal pier. The ferryboat had strings of brightly coloured flags in the rigging and looked very smart as she steamed down the Sommerdal Fjord, round the lighthouse on the point, past the waterfall and Bog Island and through The Narrows into Gloomifjord.

19

When everyone was ashore on the pier they all lined up with the Gloomifjord people behind huge Norwegian flags carried by Daddy, Farmer Brattbakk, Mr Uphouse the schoolmaster, Mr Kraftlag the handyman and the other menfolk. Ottar banged his drum and the school band started to play the National Anthem as they marched up the hill to the Youth Club Hall. Every house in the village had a Norwegian flag flying in the wind.

As the band passed Grampa Gloomifjord's house, Brita looked up and saw him sitting on the roof, holding on to the chimney pot, waving his flag and cheering at the top of his voice.

"I wish he wouldn't go up there," said Mum. "It doesn't look safe."

When they reached the hall, Brita was in the choir to sing the 'Yes, We Love This Country' song – the National Anthem. Everyone clapped and then Mr Storting, the Member of Parliament, stood up to make a speech.

"We should all be very proud today," he began, "for to be born a Norwegian is a wonderful achievement and you children should never forget it."

20

"Mum," whispered Brita. "Where's Grampa? He's not here yet. Shall I go and see?"

"Perhaps you should," said Mum, but Ottar had already tiptoed to the back door of the hall and was looking back down the hill to Grampa's house. Brita followed him.

"Why's Grampa still cheering and waving his flag up on the roof?" she asked.

"He's not. He's shouting for help," said Ottar.

"Yes, you should all be proud," Mr Storting was saying, "proud to be such brave, caring, hard-working, modest and patriotic people!"

"Excuse me, Mr Storting," said Brita, "I'm sorry to interrupt you but our Grampa's stuck on the roof of his house!"

Daddy and Mr Storting rushed to the door, followed by Hans Tufte and Farmer Nils Brattbakk. They all ran down the hill to Grampa's house.

21

"What's wrong?" Daddy called.

"It's the ladder. The wind blew it over. I'm stuck!" cried Grampa.

"Don't panic! We'll soon get you down," shouted Hans Tufte. He and Daddy picked up the ladder and held it in place so Grampa could climb down

"Are you all right, Grampa?" asked Brita.

"A bit cold and shaky, my dear but, yes, I'm fine," said Grampa. "Now let's hurry to the hall or we'll miss the big dinner… Oh, it's you, Mr Storting. What did you say in your speech?"

"Well, I was just saying how patriotic we all are," said Mr Storting.

"Please, Mr Storting, what does patriotic mean?" asked Brita.

"It means you love your country," said Mr Storting.

"Oh, I know a song about that," said Brita, and she sang it as they walked back up to the hall.

> *"Yes, we love with fond devotion*
> *This, the land that looms*
> *Rugged, storm-scarred, o'er the ocean,*
> *With her thousand homes!" **

"As I was saying," Mr Storting told the crowd, "we are all very patriotic. And what better proof of that than our friend here," he said, pointing at Grampa Gloomifjord, "who risked life and limb to display our national flag on his chimney pot and got stuck as a result?"

Everybody clapped and cheered. Then the school children sang the 'Yes, We Love This Country' anthem once more, Mum and her friends did a traditional folk dance, and Hans Tufte and his band played their accordions while everyone else sat down to a huge National Day feast.

Afterwards there was a dance. Ottar danced with Mum who showed him where to put his feet. Brita danced with Daddy who joked that he was steering her round the dance floor just like he steered his ship. And Grampa Gloomifjord danced with Miss Tufte, the post lady.

"That was a silly thing to do, getting stuck on the roof," Miss Tufte said.

"Ah, well, you see, that's what comes of me being so patriotic!" said Grampa.

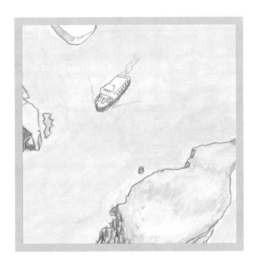

*   In Norwegian they sing it like this:

> *Ja, vi elsker dette landet*
> *Som det stiger frem*
> *Furet, vaerbitt over vannet,*
> *Med de tusen hjem…*

23

The Gloomifjord Birds and the Berries

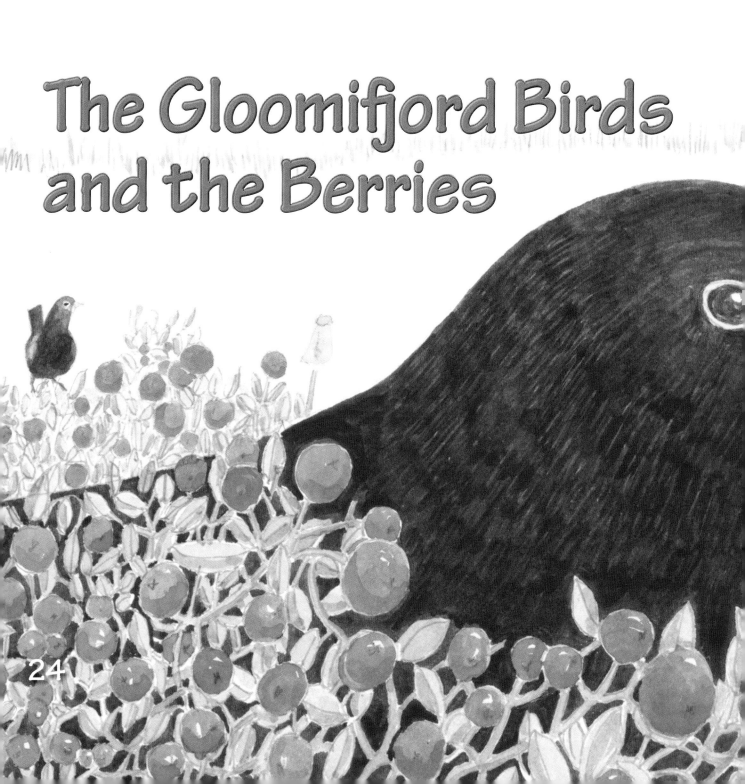

24

25

It was a sunny Saturday morning in Sommerdal. The twins, Ottar and Brita, were getting ready to go to visit Grampa in Gloomifjord with their Mum.

"Why not ring him up first to see if there's anything he needs us to take on the bus?" said Mum. So they did.

"Haa-lo, Grampa!" said Brita. "How are you today?"

"Oh, not so good," said Grampa Gloomifjord.

"What's wrong, Grampa?" asked Brita.

"Oh, it's the birds, the blackbirds, you know. They're eating all the berries on the bushes in my garden," said Grampa Gloomifjord. "I wonder if you could bring over some netting."

"We will," said Brita.

So Mum took the twins into the gardening department of Mrs Whalewick's shop. Mrs Whalewick said she was sorry but everyone had been buying netting to keep the blackbirds off their berry bushes and she'd none left.

"I don't know if it's worth ordering any more," she sighed. "Folk just buy it as soon as it comes in, and then we have none again."

"Oh dear, what are we going to do?" asked Brita as they walked past the fish factory pier on their way home.

"There's some netting!" said Ottar. "Look! There's a big pile of it on the pier by Skipper Norstein's fishing boat."

"I wonder if he'd let us have an old bit," said Mum. "Come on, let's ask him." And so they did.

"You've come at the right time," said Skipper Norstein. "We've just been told to dump this. It's a perfectly good net but the Government says we've got to use one with bigger meshes in it, so the little fish can escape through the holes more easily and more of them will grow up to be big fish before we catch them. It's called conservation, I think."

"We only need a little bit, to keep the birds off Grampa's berry bushes," said Brita.

"No problem. I'll cut a piece out for you," smiled Skipper Norstein, taking a very sharp knife from his belt. "And do give your Grampa my best wishes when you see him."

He cut out a huge piece of net. They rolled it up into a long sausage and tied it with string. Ottar took one end, Brita took the other and, with Mum holding up the middle of the parcel, they managed to get it onto Mr Murkidal's bus.

"Going fishing?" said Mr Murkidal.

The bus purred along the valley, up the hill, through the woods and into the Gloomifjord Tunnel. It was a long tunnel and very dark. Ottar held Mum's hand in case the tunnel trolls got him. But they didn't.

Suddenly it was light again and they were rolling down the winding road to Gloomifjord. The bus stopped by Grampa's house.

"This," said Mr Murkidal, with a long sigh, "This - is -Gloomifjord."

Mum went into the house to make Grampa a cup of coffee while the twins set to work. They chased away the blackbirds from the berry bushes. Brita opened the long parcel and Ottar rolled out the net. They put up sticks and set jam jars on top of them. Then they hung the netting all over the sticks and jam jars, so the blackbirds couldn't get at the berries any more.

"Well, Grampa, what do you think of THAT?" asked Ottar.

Grampa Gloomifjord was so pleased he gave the twins a big hug and danced around the garden with them.

"Oh, what kind and clever bairns!" he said. "You've fixed those cheeky blackbirds!"

"But what are those big birds in the cabbage patch, Grampa?" asked Brita.

"Oh, help!" said Grampa. "It's the blooming crows again! They're eating the baby plants! Nils Brattbakk's put a bird scarer in his field to keep them off his corn and every time it goes 'bang!' the crows just fly over here. And we've used up all the netting on the berry bushes!"

27

"We could make a scarecrow of our own," said Brita. And so they did.

Mum hammered an old clothes pole into the ground and tied a broomstick across it to make the arms; Brita found a moth-eaten jacket in the shed and slid the arms through the broomstick to make the scarecrow's body; Ottar painted a scary face on a fishing float that had washed up on the beach; Mum found some old gardening gloves and tied them on to make the hands; and Grampa hung his oldest and dirtiest fishing trousers on the pole to make the legs.

"All the scarecrow needs now is a hat," said Brita.

"There's one on the beach that floated ashore after the fishing competition," said Ottar, and he ran to fetch it.

The scarecrow now looked very much like a real person standing in the cabbage patch.

"He ought to have a name, really," said Brita.

"We'll call him Mr Murkidal!" laughed Grampa. "It looks just like him with that hat!"

"How will we make Mr Murkidal go 'BANG!' like Farmer Brattbakk's bird scarer?" asked Ottar.

"Ah, that one works with a gas cylinder and it would be rather expensive just to protect a few cabbages in a garden like mine," explained Grampa. "But maybe we could make something that looks like a gun and that would frighten the crows away."

So Brita and Ottar went to look in the wood. They found a crooked piece of wood that had blown down in a gale. It looked just like a gun when they fixed it to the scarecrow. Grampa was delighted.

"That's perfect!" said Mum. "It'll take a brave crow to come anywhere near Mr Murkidal! Thank you for cheering up your Grampa."

"Is it nearly dinner time?" asked Ottar.

"It is," said Mum, "But first, let's pick some berries."

So they did. And they ate them all up with sour cream, after a big dinner of salt codfish and potatoes with melted butter poured over them, as is the custom in Gloomifjord.

The Shortest Night
in Gloomifjord

29

The Gloomifjord
Fishing Competition

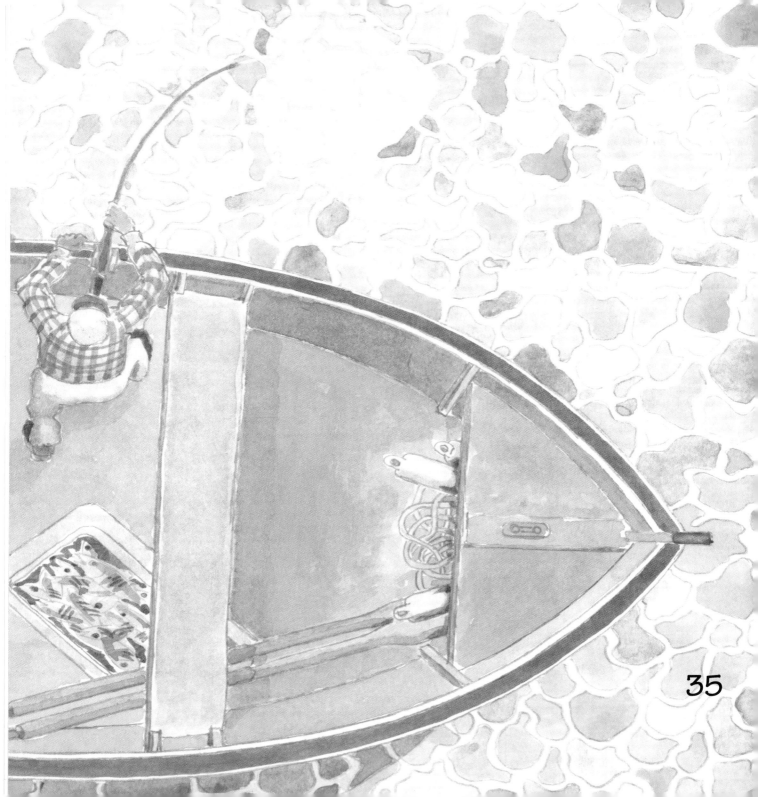

35

Grampa Gloomifjord and the Midges

 The twins were staying at Grampa Gloomifjord's house at the end of the summer holidays. The weather was warm and everybody was suntanned and cheerful. Even Grampa Gloomifjord was cheerful – until the midges came.

Brita and Ottar were playing on the beach one afternoon when they heard a strange noise, a sort of slapping sound and a loud roaring.

"Quick! It's Grampa!" said Brita. "I think he's hurt himself!"

They ran up to the house and there was Grampa, bright red in the face, dancing around the veranda and slapping himself with a wet towel.

"What's wrong, Grampa? Are you sick?" asked Ottar.

"Sick? No! But I'm sick of these blooming midges!" cried Grampa. "They're biting me all over! Even under my whiskers!"

"They're not biting us, Grampa," said Brita.

"Hah! They must like the taste of me better!" said Grampa.

"Here, put on some of Mum's insect cream," said Ottar.

So he did, but it didn't make much difference. The midges still buzzed in a cloud all around Grampa. They even followed him into the kitchen when he tried to escape.

"There's only one answer to this problem," said Grampa. "We must go fishing. At once!"

"Fishing, Grampa?" said the twins. "But how will that help?"

"You'll see," said Grampa. "Now put your lifejackets on and help me get the boat ready."

Under Grampa's house his little red boat was sitting in the summer dock. He started the old 'bung bung' engine and they chugged out onto the calm waters of Gloomifjord. The midges followed Grampa's head for a little way but then they turned and buzzed back to the shore.

"See?" said Grampa. "That always works! Now, let's catch some fish before your mother comes back from Bergen with the shopping."

Grampa gave the twins fishing rods and soon they started catching things. Ottar caught an old welly boot. Brita caught a shopping basket from Mrs Whalewick's shop.

41

"That'll be handy to put the fish in when we catch them," said Grampa, as he hauled in the minister's umbrella that had blown away on the day of the Great Gale of Gloomifjord.

After a while he said: "Hmph! No midges here, but no fish either. Let's go a little further out. We'll see your mother coming in on the ferry so we won't miss her."

Out in the deeper water they didn't catch anything at all. For two whole hours. It was very warm, even when the sun went behind a big black cloud.

"Look! There's the Bergen ferry coming round the point, Grampa!" said Brita. "We'd better go home now."

"FISH! FISH!" roared Grampa, as his fishing rod suddenly bent double.

"WOW!" shouted Ottar, as his rod did the same and tried to pull him over the side of the boat.

"HELP!" cried Brita, as she felt a huge weight twitching on her fishing line.

Grampa reeled in his fish as fast as he could. Soon there were six wet mackerel flapping around the bottom of the boat and tangling up the fishing line. Then he helped Ottar haul in his catch. When he'd helped Brita to land her fish there were eighteen mackerel in a shiny heap in the shopping basket.

42

The twins held up some of the fish to show Mum as the Bergen ferry steamed past them.

"Look, Mum! We got six each!" they called.

"Time to come ashore now!" Mum shouted. "I've got something for Grampa!"

"Hmph! Back to those blooming midges," grumbled Grampa Gloomifjord, but he started the motor and the twins took turns to steer the boat back to the dock. As they glided into the boat's house under Grampa's kitchen, there was an enormous FLASH that lit up both sides of Gloomifjord and then, only a little while later, a very loud "BANG!"

"Is it the engine, Grampa?" asked Ottar.

"No, no! It's a thunderstorm," cried Grampa. "How splendid! This'll make the potatoes grow AND sort out the midges!"

Just then the rain came pelting down. They hurried up to the kitchen with the basket of fish. Grampa gutted them and they had the mackerel frying by the time Mum came up from the ferry pier. She was carrying a parcel.

"This is for you, Dad," she said. "The midges will be here any day now."

"Hmph! You're a bit late," said Grampa. "They're here already!"

"Open your present, Grampa, and don't be so grumpy," said Brita.

So he did, and inside the parcel was the oddest hat you ever saw. It had a veil of fine net that covered Grampa's head down to his shoulders.

"You look like an explorer in the jungle!" laughed Ottar.

"Doesn't he just?" said Mum. "I saw it in the sports shop in Bergen. It's called a Bugwear hat and it's really for keeping the mosquitoes off you if you go to Africa, but it ought to work just as well on midges here in Norway. You always suffer so when they come, Dad."

"I'll try it out," said Grampa, and he went to the door. Then he stopped: "Oh, dear," he said. "I forgot. It's raining and the midges will have gone. What a pity!"

"Oh, what a grumpy old Grampa you are today," smiled Brita. And she gave him a big kiss, right on top of his new Bugwear hat.

44

Grampa
Gloomifjord and
the Birthday Pier

"Haa-lo Grampa!" said Brita. "How are you today?"

"Oh, not so good, I'm afraid," replied Grampa Gloomifjord. "You see, my pier is falling down."

"But half of your house is standing on top of the pier," said Brita.

"I know," said Grampa. "The council sent me a letter to say I have to make it safe or I'll have to leave the house because it's too dangerous for me to stay."

"Oh dear, Grampa, that's terrible! We'll have to think of something!" said Brita, and she went to talk to Mum.

"Yes, it's true, Brita," said Mum. "The councillors are trying to help but it's quite unusual for people to live on top of piers and they're not sure if they can find money for it. They'd have to bring special pier builders from Bergen and it could be quite expensive. Of course, Daddy and I will help but, even so, we may not be able to afford it."

Brita told Ottar about the problem.

"The pier's made of wood, isn't it?" he asked.

"Yes," said Brita.

"Well, then," said Ottar, "Farmer Brattbakk has lots of logs laid by, doesn't he?"

"He does. And they're as big as some of the logs in Grampa's pier…"

"So," said Ottar, "We ask Farmer Brattbakk to help and he will because he's Grampa's friend and he'll ask some of the fishing competition people to help too."

"But we'll need a big crane to lift the logs, Ottar. They're very heavy," said Brita.

"Well, maybe the councillors would let Grampa use their crane," said Ottar. "After all, he lets everyone use his pier, doesn't he?"

"He does," said Brita. "It's really the people's pier."

45

When Daddy came home from sea next day and heard the news he was very worried. He got on the phone to the Gloomifjord people and the council at once. By dinner time he was looking more cheerful: "That was a very good idea of yours, Ottar," he said. "I think I've got most of it arranged. We'll try to make a start on it next Saturday. I don't have to go back to sea for a month so we'll see how we get on."

And so they went to work. Farmer Brattbakk and the Gloomifjord Horse hauled logs down from the Helly Woods; the fishing competition men came with their boats and towed the logs over to the pier; and Mr Uphouse the schoolmaster, who'd been a lumberjack before he went to teacher training college, brought his special woodwork tools down to Grampa's and cut the logs to the right shape so they could be bolted together.

After a while a man from the council came along and asked if they had permission.

"Yes, I myself gave permission," said Grampa. "We're mending my pier, so I don't need anyone's permission. But we do need a crane."

The council man said he would see what he could do, but just then Skipper Norstein steamed into the fjord with his fishing boat, which had a very big crane that could lift the heaviest logs.

Grampa was delighted. He kept interfering and giving orders, but the men just laughed and told him to fetch another pot of coffee. The twins handed hammers and nuts and bolts to the pier menders and helped Mum make sandwiches and cakes. It was all more like a big, jolly picnic than hard work.

After three weekends the job was finished. Grampa invited everyone who'd helped him to come to a big barbecue with cod's head soup and pickled herring and as many goats' cheese sandwiches as they could eat. After a little glass of Farmer Brattbakk's apple cider, Grampa made a speech:

"My friends," he said. "When I found out that my pier was falling to bits I was very sad. I feared I would have to go and live at the old people's houses in Sommerdal. I'm told it's very pleasant there but I'm not ready for that just yet. So, thanks to your kindness, I can stay where I am.

46

"I can never pay you in money because I haven't got any but, if ever you want any vegetables from the garden or fish from my boat…"

"Or goats' cheese!" whispered Ottar.

"Or goats' cheese, indeed, then you only have to ask," said Grampa.

"Hooray!" shouted the pier menders and, after a few more cups of coffee and blueberry cakes, off home they all went.

Next morning Grampa said: "Oh, dear, it's going to be a bit quiet next weekend."

"That'll make a change, Grampa," said Brita. "You need a rest."

Later, Brita told Ottar she was almost sure Grampa had forgotten next Saturday was his 70th birthday. They told Mum and she said she thought the same. "Let's surprise him," she said, and then spent the whole evening on the phone.

Next Saturday morning, when the twins and Mum went over to Gloomifjord on the bus, they found Grampa picking some lettuces and spring onions in his garden.

"Just some salad stuff for Skipper Norstein's wife," he said.

"I'll help you, Grampa," said Brita. She put the greens in a basket while Mum and Ottar went into the house to make coffee and put the birthday presents out on the veranda.

"You know, Mum, he really has forgotten it's his birthday," Ottar whispered.

At coffee time they called Grampa in. When he'd washed the earth off his hands he sat down at the kitchen table.

"Er, where's the coffee?" he asked.

"It's out on the veranda on your new pier," said Mum. "Come and see."

As Grampa opened the door to the veranda he saw:

- The coffee pot, the milk jug and the coffee cups;
- A cake with 'Happy 70th Birthday' written on it, in chocolate coffee icing;
- His birthday cards and presents;
- All his friends standing in their boats, moored in a half-circle round the end of the new pier.

"Happy Birthday to You!" they sang, "Happy Birthday to You…"

"Good heavens! I'd forgotten all about it," said Grampa. "What a lovely surprise! How old did you say I was?"

"Oh, Grampa!" laughed Brita.

"…Happy Birthday to You - hoo!" sang the people in the boats.

Luckily, it was a very, very big cake.

48

The Snowy Day in Gloomifjord

49

It was Friday evening in Sommerdal. The twins were nearly ready for bed when Ottar peeped out of the window to see if he could see the moon.

"Look, Brita! It's snowing!" he said.

"Let's phone Grampa Gloomifjord!" said Brita.

"Haa-lo, Grampa! It's snowing here. Is it snowing in Gloomifjord too?" asked Ottar.

"Oh, yes, I'm sorry to say it is. Isn't this just terrible?" said Grampa Gloomifjord.

"No! It's wonderful, you silly old Grampa!" said Ottar. "We're going to bring our skis when we come to see you tomorrow."

"Oh dear. Do be careful now," said Grampa.

It snowed and blew a gale of wind all night but in the morning it was sunny and frosty as they made ready to go to Gloomifjord.

"It's such a lovely day, I think we should ski all the way to Grampa's," said Mum at breakfast time. "I believe the ski tow's working so we can get a lift to the top of the Hill of Trolls and then ski down the old track to Gloomifjord."

"Hooray!" cried the twins, and went to look for their cross-country ski shoes.

The ski tow was really just Farmer Nils Brattbakk's old snow tractor. He was going up to the top of the Helly Woods to bring down some logs for the fire. He hitched a long rope on to the back of the tractor and pulled Mum and the twins up the slope.

From the top of the woods they could see all the way down into Sommerdal, on the sunny side of the Hill of Trolls, and all the way down into Gloomifjord on the shady side.

"Whee!" cried Brita as she whizzed down the hill.

"Wow!" shouted Ottar as he swished along in her tracks.

50 "Whoa!" said Mum. "You bairns are too fast for me!"

At the bottom of the hill there was an enormous snowdrift at the edge of the fjord. Sticking out of the top of it were a chimney and a bit of roof.

"Ottar," said Brita. "Where's Grampa's house gone?"

"Oh dear," said Ottar. "I think it's under the snow. Mum! Come quickly!"

Just then they heard a voice from the chimney pot:

"Is that you, twins? Help!" said the voice.

"Don't worry, Grampa!" said Ottar. "We'll soon dig you out!"

Mum went and got shovels from the neighbours and they started to dig. Miss Tufte the post lady stopped to help and then Mr Uphouse the schoolteacher and Mr Kraftlag the handyman and Mrs Rundupp the gardener and Mr Woodwick the harbourmaster all came to lend a hand as well.

When they'd dug a tunnel to the front door, Mum went in to make Grampa a cup of coffee and made sure he hadn't lost the pills he had to take for his weakness.

Miss Tufte said it was the worst snow they'd had in Gloomifjord since the old days but then they always got the worst of the weather in Gloomifjord and those Sommerdal folk really had no idea what bad weather was like, living as they did on that rich land over on the sunny side of the hill. Grampa nodded his head in a gloomy sort of way.

"Now, bairns," said Mum. "Your poor Grampa's had a bad night of it so I'm going to light the stove and make him some hot porridge. You dig a path to the shed and get some logs and then we'll see if we can cheer him up."

"I know how to cheer him up," said Brita.

Soon the fire was crackling and Grampa had put on the special winter woolly cardigan Mum knitted for him last Christmas and he was eating the special little cakes she'd brought from Sommerdal and warmed on the stove.

"More cheerful now, Dad?" asked Mum.

51

"Hmm…" said Grampa.

Just then there came a tap, tap, tap on the window. It was Brita.

"Grampa! Grampa! Come and see! Come and see!" she shouted.

Grampa rubbed a clear space on the frosty windowpane and looked out - into the face of a snowman the same size as him. In fact, the snowman looked surprisingly like Grampa. He was even wearing his old hat and scarf. Next to the snowman was a little house made of snowballs, with a candle burning inside it.

"Ah, such kind and clever bairns!" he said. "And the snowman doesn't seem to mind the cold at all!"

"He likes it!" said Brita.

The Brightest Light in Gloomifjord

December had come around again and the Sommerdal twins were on the phone to Grampa Gloomifjord:

"Haa-lo, Grampa!" said Brita. "What are you doing today?"

"Oh, just reading a book, as usual," said Grampa Gloomifjord.

"What's it about?" asked Brita.

"Oh, you know, about the old days in Gloomifjord, long ago, when I was young and strong and happy."

"Aren't you happy now, Grampa?" said Brita.

"Well, it's just that it's very dark here on a north-facing slope in the middle of winter and that's so-o depressing, you know," said Grampa Gloomifjord.

"What you need is a more cheerful story book," said Brita.

"I suppose so, but my eyesight's not so good and the light in this house is very dim so I can't even read for long," said Grampa.

"Never mind, Grampa," said Brita, "We're coming over for Christmas next week and we'll have fun every day."

When Daddy came home from the sea for Christmas, Brita and Ottar told him about Grampa being so gloomy.

"Ah, yes, I know what you mean," said Daddy. "I was reading in the Bergen newspaper about how the winter darkness makes some people very sad. And it said one way to make them happier is to give them lots and lots of light, very bright light."

"We could buy Grampa a nice reading lamp for his Christmas," said Ottar.

"That's a very good idea. Let's go and see what they've got in the shop," said Mum.

The electrical department in Mrs Whalewick's shop was very old, very small and very cluttered.

"Please, Mrs Whalewick, we need a bright light to make Grampa happy, like he was when he was young and strong," said Brita.

"Hmmm," said Mrs Whalewick, "How about this? It's called a Petromax. There was one in every house in Gloomifjord when your Grampa was a lad." And she took out an old paraffin pressure lamp. She struck a match and lit a wick under the glass bowl. Then she started pumping a handle on the side of the paraffin tank. Suddenly the lamp lit up and started to make a hissing noise. It was very, very bright.

"Oh, it's lovely!" said Brita. "And it's warm, too!"

"Yes," said Mum, "but it's very smelly to work with paraffin and it might be dangerous. What if Grampa forgot to turn it off at night and the house went on fire?"

"Well, how about this one, then?" said Mrs Whalewick. She brought out from under the counter an old-fashioned electric table lamp with a frilly lampshade. When she switched it on there was a lovely yellow glow, but much less light than from the paraffin lamp.

"I'm sorry, it's not bright enough," said Brita.

"I think what we're really looking for, Mrs Whalewick, is what they call a 'sad lamp,'" said Daddy.

"Ah! Yes! The wonderful new Sadlite! As it happens, I've got one in stock. It came from Bergen only yesterday. Now let me see where I put it," said Mrs Whalewick. She climbed up a stepladder and brought down a shiny new box. Inside the box was a shiny new desk lamp. When she plugged it in, it lit up the dingy old shop with the most beautiful, radiant light.

"That's perfect," said Daddy. "We'll take it."

"Well, I suppose you can, but it means I won't have another one to sell," sighed Mrs Whalewick.

"And some Christmas wrapping paper too, please," said Daddy.

In Gloomifjord it is the custom to give presents on Christmas Eve, not on Christmas Morning so, when they were all gathered round the log fire at Grampa's house, Mum gave Grampa his Christmas present from her. It was a book about the old days on the Bergen ferry and the digging of the Gloomifjord Tunnel.

"What a pity! I can't see to read it in this light," grumbled Grampa. "But thank you anyway."

55

"Open OUR present now, Grampa!" shouted the twins. So he did. And when he set the Sadlite down on his reading table and switched it on, a big smile spread all over his face.

"This is wonderful!" he said. "Oh, what kind and clever bairns! I haven't seen a light that bright since the old Petromax lamps we had when I was a lad. I'm absolutely de-LIGHT-ed!"

He was so delighted that he sat down to read his new book at once. He read for hours, chuckling at the stories about the old ferryboat skippers and pointing to photographs of Gloomifjord people he remembered from long ago when he was young and strong and happy. It was almost midnight when Mum at last persuaded him to switch off the Sadlite and go to bed.

Next morning he was the happiest Grampa anyone could wish for.

"Merry Christmas! I shall keep that light on all winter!" he said.

He did. And do you know what? He was as happy as happy could be, with never a grumpy look or a gloomy word.

The End